SKIN

AN EROTIC HORROR STORY

AUDREY RUSH

Skin: A Horror Story by Audrey Rush

Independently Published

Cover Design by Kai

Amazon ISBN: 9798856346786
Barnes & Noble ISBN: 9798369298725

AUTHOR'S NOTE

This is a *horror* story. It contains disturbing sexual content, including but *not* limited to graphic violence, rape, incest, and necrophilia. A detailed list of content can be found on the author's website.

Reader discretion is advised.

SKIN

CHAPTER 1

I CRUSH THE HEAD OF MY DICK LIKE A STRESS BALL AS THE VIDEO zooms in closer to the woman's face. Her snarl transforms into a desperate cry. She twists, fighting to survive. Brown hair is matted to her temples with sweat and grime. Still, she grits her teeth and pushes herself back to keep the rope around her neck from cutting into her windpipe. A black-gloved hand grips the rope, pulling the noose taut, and terror crawls over her eyes. She knows she's not getting out of this. I stretch the skin of my balls as the rope goes tighter around her throat. Her face bulges red. A blood vessel bursts in her eye. Red veins splatter across the sclera like modern art. Her whole body twitches, reaching desperately for that last breath of air.

I bet her pussy is tightest right then.

Her eyelashes flutter like the wings of a dying insect, and my dick convulses. Jizz erupts from the tip and drips over my clenched fist.

My cock jolts with the last spurt of come. Then I wipe my hand with a tissue, cleaning the sticky clumps of semen as if it's loose clay. I sigh deeply and stare at my spare laptop again. The camera pulls back, panning over the limp body. With the corpse stretched out in the woods, it resembles a deer carcass. Red scratches are carved deep into the sides from where it struggled, but it doesn't feel anything now.

I used to wonder why snuff films were always in the woods. Then I figured it must be easier to get rid of the bodies if you film their deaths exactly where you bury them. With dense trees, it's nearly impossible to figure out where it's recorded. Law enforcement would have a hell of a time with the footage.

Not that I give a shit. Even if sick fucks like me hadn't stumbled—or searched—for this kind of video, the bitch would still be dead. Denying my orgasm wasn't going to save her life.

I exit out of the dark web and the encryption software, then log out of the VPN. I click through the settings until the entire laptop begins wiping its memory clean. It's my ritual. I don't have any friends or family I keep in contact with, but you can never be too careful with these sorts of interests.

With a clear head, I go back to work. The air in the garage is still and dank, the metallic scent of animal blood pungent in the air. Hunting season is past, so it's back to pets again. Hamsters. Lizards. Cats. So many goddamn cats. Sometimes, the large dogs keep my urges quiet for a while, but I never stop counting down the days to hunting season. I prefer big game animals. There's more of a challenge in preserving them.

On the table, the hide of a tabby cat is stretched out, salted and dried, ready for the form. I pick through the drawer of glass eyes. They go in first. Green. Brown. Honey. Even blue. I select two black ones, then form clay to the sockets. My thumbs jam the glass spheres into the soft material.

The doorbell rings.

That's the shitty thing about living where you work. It's after hours, and I never talk directly to the customers unless it's Wednesday—intake day. There's even a sign near the doorbell that directs visitors to my website's request form. And yet every once in a while, some pet owner gets particularly feverish about preserving their dead animal. They ring, and they ring, and they're met with silence. Eventually, they get the picture.

You never see hunters act like that. They know the drill.

The doorbell chimes three times in a row. I grunt, then click through the apps on my phone until I pull up the security camera attached to the doorbell. On the screen, the fisheye view shows a middle-aged woman standing on the porch. She wipes her nose, the crinkly sniffles popping through the microphone. Blond-white hair. Probably blue eyes. A long-sleeved blazer clings to her arms. She's professional. Well-kept. From this angle, she's attractive, the kind of woman that knows she looks good naked. The expensive type. Rich bitches don't usually get attached to their pets. When someone else takes care of them for you, there's no need to mourn when they die.

So why is she here?

Then I see the cardboard box, which is the size of a refrigerator, on the metal appliance dolly next to her.

She presses the doorbell again.

Curiosity sparks in my chest, clawing its way to my shoulders. I squint my eyes at the video feed, then zoom in on the box. It's too small to be an actual refrigerator. It's flatter than one too. No... It's more like a box for the unconstructed parts of a dinner table.

I'm not expecting any supplies or deliveries. She must want me to stuff something.

For a split second, I imagine a human. Her dead husband in the cardboard box. Naked and blue, his eyes sunken and cloudy.

"Hello?" the woman asks, her voice scratching through the speaker. Then she pounds her fist on the door. "Theodore Wright? I'm looking for Theodore Wright. Hello? Are you in there?"

I shake those thoughts away. I've had a lot of strange requests in this career, but I've also surfed the dark web long enough to know that the most morbid shit doesn't happen in places like this. It happens in the woods. Places where people can't see unless you *want* them to. I live in the city, where we're surrounded by an audience, where we all have to face judgment.

Make her fill out the form online, my brain instructs. *Just like everyone else. You can use the speaker on the doorbell to tell her.*

I wipe the gray grime onto a rag, little spots of clay still sticking to the webs between my fingers. I step closer to the front door.

It's not a human, my mind screams. *You're making a mistake. She's using that oversized box to lure you in. You're on a watch list, and this is the bait to see if you'll break the law. Don't fall for it, you fucking idiot.*

Need prickles inside of me, drawing me closer to the entrance.

What's in the box?

I open the door.

"Oh!" She startles, then immediately grabs the dolly and rolls it closer to me. Her sleeves pull up on her arms, exposing red, scaly skin, evidence that she's been scratching the surface, clawing for a way inside. An SUV is parked on the street, a man waiting behind the wheel.

"Come back on Wednesday," I say. "That's when I do the intake. There's a form online—"

Her body collides with mine abruptly, and her heat closes in on me so fast that I instantly lurch back.

She goes past me, wheeling the box inside.

"Please," she begs. "It's my daughter."

CHAPTER 2

HER DAUGHTER?

Once the woman is past me, I adjust my pants, hoping that none of the clumps of clay are on the fabric, making my semi-erection noticeable. I clear my throat and ready myself for a real conversation.

"Daughter" doesn't mean anything. Pet owners like to say "fur babies" for a reason, and I've heard some of them use the terms "daughter" and "son" as well. It could be a pet chimpanzee or a miniature horse for all I know.

A sob escapes the woman's lips. My upper lip curls in disgust. Whatever is in the box, she must have been close with it.

I gesture to the dolly, silently signaling that I'll move it. As she passes it off to me, our hands touch. My stomach tenses. She's invading my space, and hatred wells inside of me. It burns me from the inside out. She wouldn't like it if I crawled into her midtown penthouse, and yet she shoves herself inside of my home with her box like she owns the place.

My vision takes hold of the box. I focus on it.

That is why I let her in here, I tell myself. I need to know.

The dolly isn't as heavy as I thought it would be. It's heavier than a chimp and lighter than a horse. The guessing game continues.

It's going to be a letdown, my brain warns. *You're getting excited for nothing.*

I swallow those thoughts down and take the box to the dinner table. It's the only surface that's clean right now.

In the end, this is work.

"My husband said you can help us," the woman says quietly. I hoist the box onto the table, and she reaches forward to help me. Getting in the way. Intruding again. I let her so she'll get it over with, and our shoulders briefly touch. My skin crawls with invisible insects at her proximity. "He said you're the best in the region."

I stand back from the table and blink slowly. I *am* skilled. It helps when you start your craft in elementary school. When I was seven, I had snuck into my sister's room and took her pet mouse. It was so eager in my hands, ready to escape. It thrashed and burrowed into my palms, and when those tiny incisors had locked onto my skin, I dropped it. It scurried away and hid under the bed.

Anger had filled me then. That little shit wasn't going to bite me like that and get away with it. So I crawled under the bed. Trapped it in a corner. And this time, when I caught it, I didn't let go. Fascination had replaced anger, and I held my breath too, waiting to see who would die from oxygen loss first: me or the mouse.

Survival had kicked in. I inhaled, savoring the air, even at that young age. It was then that I realized the mouse had stopped moving.

I opened my palms. It was dead.

Guilt had filtered through my veins. My sister was the only one in our family who was nice to me. We knew what it was like to live in a cold house, and she had rescued that mouse from a trap in the neighbor's yard.

I told her the mouse had gotten out of the cage.

It had taken hundreds of hours of watching instructional videos, but eventually, I stuffed the mouse and gave it back to her. She had cried when she saw it. Then she hit me. Repeatedly.

You killed it, didn't you? she had screamed at me. *How could you?*

I just wanted to help you, I said.

Bruises had formed from her blows, but her reaction didn't stop me from killing a squirrel. Nor from poisoning the neighbor's cat.

By the time I was in middle school, I understood that I could use my skills to hide what I was doing. No one would question my fascination with dead things if that's how I made money. And I was so good that by the time I graduated high school, I bought my own house. My sister and parents stopped talking to me then.

That didn't matter. I had my business.

While there are plenty of hobbyists in the region, there's only one licensed professional to compete with. It's why I can turn away customers after hours. It's why I don't have to bend to their demands.

So why am I bending to hers?

"Well, are you the best?" the woman asks.

I sneer. I shouldn't have let her in here. I know that. Even when you don't say a word, people see things, and it's like taking off my shell and showing her the destroyed flesh underneath. Inviting her to be my dissector.

"I am," I say.

My eyes gloss over the cardboard box. Blood trickles to my groin. That disgust melts away as I imagine the possibilities.

"What is it?" I ask.

She shakes her head, then points at the box. "Please. I can't look at her like that."

Her.

My forehead lifts. I peel the brown lid off the corner, barely exposing the object inside. An eyebrow. Pale skin. Then a face. A woman—young enough to be her daughter, yet old enough to be a student at the college—lies flat like a child tucked in a bed. Cold fog rises from the skin. It has blond hair, and though there are decades between them, the resemblance is clear.

It really is the woman's daughter.

"My baby," the Mother whispers.

My dick twitches and pushes against my pants. I sit down in the nearest chair, hiding my erection, then I reach over and pull

7

back the lid some more. Sitting at this angle, I can see deeper into the box. An exposed tit. A nipple. No visible marks of trauma on the body.

Unmarked.

Both of them—the Mother and the Daughter—are attractive versions of one another, and though I'd gladly fuck the Mother to get rid of my erection, there's a simplicity to the Daughter's expression that attracts me. The untarnished body, not yet burdened by years of abuse. A cool tint clings to the skin, like a porcelain so white that it curls into the softest blue.

"How long?" I ask.

The Mother closes her eyes, pain clenched in her temples.

"We found her like that yesterday morning," she says raggedly. "My husband. He——" She pauses, then looks away. "My husband wanted to take care of her himself, but I insisted we go to a professional. It's what she would have wanted. It's what she deserves."

My brows scrunch. I stay focused on the body. Dead things are familiar. There's nothing they can do to scare you. Even when the natural gasses gurgle in obnoxious farts, they don't fight. They're dead. There's nothing left for them to do. It's called an inanimate object for a reason. It doesn't have a preference.

She doesn't deserve anything. She is an *it*.

I use the same words as the Mother to make it more comfortable for us and get the interaction over with as quickly as possible.

"How did she die?"

The Mother sniffles, and those sobs drown out the sound of my palm skimming across my pants, stroking my dick underneath the table. What a waste of life. There's no fight. And even if there was, the Mother probably put makeup on the corpse, unable to acknowledge that final reality for herself.

"The medical examiner said it was an overdose," the Mother says, her voice quivering. "I just don't know why she'd do that to herself. She was such a good girl. Happy. Smart. We couldn't have asked for a better daughter, you know? It doesn't make sense…"

The Mother's voice whistles away, droning on about the Daughter's potential. People lose their goddamn minds when their pet dies; they're annoying. It's why I only do intakes once a week now.

The Mother's mouth contorts as she speaks, and I realize there's something different about this. It's not the fact that the Daughter is more than a pet. It's that the Mother seems to feel guilt. As if she believes it's her fault that the Daughter died. That she was a part of the overdose somehow.

My eyes focus on the Mother, but it's not her current state that I see. I imagine the Mother's mouth twisting into a scream. My dick becomes a knife, jabbing that warm pussy, and her body is frantic as she punches my jaw, desperate to live, even as her eyes show that she knows it's hopeless. A cunt like her *will* die for me.

"Do you know what I mean?" the Mother asks.

I blink. Hard. Sometimes, my daydreams get the best of me. It's not that I *want* to hurt others; it's that I can't stop the visions of imagining what it would be like. The struggle. The rancid fear. The raw anger. The salty taste of freedom. Of blood. The adrenaline filling my cock so full that the skin bursts like a balloon. It's like my brain unfurls, and there's no way to put the thoughts back inside.

This time, I jerk myself away from the Mother until I'm staring at the table. My eyes drift, and even though I know I shouldn't, I focus on the exposed face and shoulder of the corpse, the shadowed, blue-gray clavicle.

"She was so young," the Mother cries.

I roll my eyes. This isn't about the Daughter, is it? The body before us is an extension of the Mother. Her literal flesh and blood. Perhaps the Mother is facing her own mortality for the first time, proof that one day, she will die too. Her emotions have nothing to do with the Daughter and everything to do with the fact that the Mother lives on *beyond* the Daughter. The guilt associated with survival.

"Why not get it embalmed?" I ask.

"The mortician said he——" Her lips pinch into a thin line. "He was too much of a rule follower. He said we couldn't keep her. That there are laws he has to follow. He wouldn't let us mourn our way."

I tune her out and stare at the corpse. Light orange freckles—almost green with that cool tint—crest the bridge of the Daughter's nose. Jasmine faintly wafts from the hair. Perhaps the hair was recently shampooed. A smile tugs at my lips. It's like she wanted to be presentable in death.

Based on the freckles, the Daughter might've been a natural redhead before she started dying her hair blond. Who dyed their hair first: the Mother or the Daughter? There must not have been any separation between them. An unhealthy relationship. Love becomes obsession, and obsession is never safe. It's why I'm alone. It's why the Mother is here.

I don't have to hear her formal request. We both know what she wants: to give a second life to her precious child. Her mini-me.

What does the Father think of an obsession like this?

Our way, she had said. The obsession may run deeper than a maternal bond.

My gaze fixes on the corpse. An overdose means she died easily, but for a few seconds, I pretend what it must have felt like when she died. Her body loose and limp as her last breath dispersed into the air.

I shouldn't be doing this. *I can't.* Dealing with a human body is a liability, and doing business with a woman like this is a mistake. I'm going to get caught, and then I'll spend the rest of my life in prison. They won't let you jerk off to snuff films or stuff dead animals behind bars.

I suck in through my nose, that sweet scent of death filling my nostrils. It's so close, though. So fucking close, I could reach out and take the dead cunt right now if I wanted.

I rip my eyes away from the body and face the woman.

"It's illegal," I say. "It's toxic waste now."

Tears fill the Mother's eyes. Then hostility takes over as she grits her teeth. "My daughter is not *toxic waste.*"

I tilt my gaze from the Mother to the wall behind her and try to ignore the body in front of me.

It's no use. My eyes gravitate to the corpse.

Toxic waste.

I don't like looking into people's eyes. They see things. They know when you're hiding something. But a corpse? It's an object. Even with taxidermied animals, there's nothing there. No worries. No judgment. No sorrow or shame or guilt. They become decorations. You give them personalities. You make up their lives.

"No one has to know," the Mother begs. "Please——" She fumbles through her purse. "I have money. Lots of it——"

Preserving the Daughter would be a challenge. And with the looks of her, the Mother has enough money to pay a full year's salary for one stuffing.

But you can't send a human hide to get tanned.

I grimace. What's wrong with me? This corpse—the Daughter —is not an animal. If the city regulators find out what I'm doing, I'll lose my license. End my career. Strip myself of the life I've built.

There are too many people involved. The Mother, the Father, and me.

At least the Daughter is already dead. And it's not like I killed her.

I scrunch my eyes shut. I can't give in.

"I don't taxidermize humans," I say.

"Please," the Mother says. "I just——" She shudders profusely. "I can't——"

"I don't taxidermize humans," I repeat.

The Mother throws her arms around me, her warmth suffocating, and I'm trapped in her sauna. I close my eyes and imagine what it would be like to see the Mother in a film. Deep in the woods. Nowhere to run. Her body scratched with red streaks. The emptiness filling her eyes as a gloved hand slits her throat.

My eyes open, falling instantly on the Daughter's pale cheeks. The legs must be pale too, like hard butter kept in the fridge past its prime.

If my sister had died, would my mother have kept her like this?

No. My mother would have known that I couldn't be trusted near an object like that. And I know what may happen now.

It's wrong to do this. *The dead should be allowed to rest,* I tell myself. It's what society says is right. Even the snuff filmmakers know to bury the bodies.

But the Daughter is already dead. And I didn't kill her.

I pull back from the Mother's embrace.

"All right," I say.

A grotesque sob escapes the Mother's chest. "Thank you. Thank you so much." She instantly shifts, clearing her throat. "How long does it take?"

Her sudden shift in demeanor startles me. She's onto business though. I can appreciate that.

Most hides only take a few days to tan, but it can take longer, depending on the size. Truth be told, tanning is not my expertise. I'm good at stuffing. At shaping clay to fit a memory and sewing hides to conceal the seams.

"Check back in a few weeks. You have my number?"

"On your website, right? Oh!" She pulls me in for another hug. "You'll never know how grateful I am."

Her honeysuckle perfume swirls around me like a tornado, my head pulsing with nausea. It's synthetic, like the colognes I used to use to cover the smell of dead animals on my skin when I was younger. But no matter how much you spray, it's always there. Even when you try to go to college, when you go to the store, when you try to date like a normal person, the scent clings to your skin, and a primal instinct wells up inside of everyone else. That fear keeps them away from you. They make up excuses about why they can't see you again, but the truth is in their eyes. Seeing past the mask. Knowing what's underneath.

The judgmental cunts.

"This will be expensive," I say to the Mother. "And there are no guarantees."

"I know."

We discuss the terms and settle on a price. As soon as she starts telling me the Daughter's life story and how she was a good mother to her, I shove her out the front door. I watch the SUV leave from the peephole.

I close the cardboard box, then heave it through the house.

In the corner of the garage, a walk-in freezer takes up a large portion of the space. I use it for hunting season and overflow; the game animals can be big, and I can't always fit them into the chest freezers. Inside, two dog carcasses lie on the ground, ready to be skinned and shipped off for tanning. I move them to the side, then set the Daughter's cardboard coffin on the ground.

On autopilot, I open the box to check the specimen, and a wave of excitement rolls through me at seeing the naked body.

In the freezer's light, the Daughter looks gentle, as if in a dreamless sleep. Closed eyes. Loose cheeks. Her mouth slightly open. The nipples are erect, like they're sensitive from the cold. It's odd to think of a corpse having hard nipples, but only because it was human; I've seen it with other mammals.

My dick swells.

I open the eyelids and stare at the blue, milky eyes. The beautiful thing about blue and green eyes, no matter what kind of animal you are, is that you snap on a coordinated collar and that color transforms the specimen. I've seen it with cats and dogs. Some customers paint their shoulder mounts to match their decor, and suddenly, that piebald deer looks like it has leafy green eyes. And right now, the Daughter's eyes pop, matching with the icy blue metal around us.

My dick throbs as I picture the Daughter being strangled to death. Blue lingerie clinging to her small breasts. Her erect nipples pushing through the fabric the harder she struggles. Her blue eyes laced with blood vessels.

I shake the image away.

I close the cardboard box and shove it to the side, underneath the shelves. I close the door.

The Daughter is already dead. I didn't do anything wrong.

A thought is just a thought.

CHAPTER 3

THOUGHTS KEEP YOU AWAKE AT NIGHT. THOUGHTS ARE WHAT drive our brains to the depths of insanity. Thoughts are what make me jerk off closer and closer to that fucking freezer.

The lights are off. The house is dark. I stand outside of the walk-in freezer in my boxers, my dick poking out of the hole, hoping that I don't open that door.

Thoughts. It's always just a thought.

Eventually I give in and jack off before finding my way back to my bed. Sleep follows. When I return to the garage in the morning, I return to the cat I was working on yesterday and use a wet rag to clean its fur. I keep my back to the walk-in freezer. I'm almost able to forget the Daughter.

Almost.

I store the finished cat in the front room and make a mental note to schedule the pickup. Then I scan the internet for human stuffing ideas.

Naturally, I end up on an embalming website. By mixing the right chemicals, you can play god and create a somewhat plastified corpse, keeping it presentable and "lifelike" for a while longer. You can delay the decomposition process.

I've spoken with a few morticians; they sometimes use cotton in the genitals to soak up any extra liquids leftover from the insides. You can't stop the rot though. Not completely. Besides, embalming lasts for a few years at most, and from what I gathered, the Mother wants something durable and long-lasting. A way to take the Daughter on missed family vacations. Bringing the stuffed corpse along like a piece of jewelry to wear to Sunday brunch.

But with pet taxidermy, you can touch the fur. The feathers. The scales. You can feel what had been there.

I went to a funeral once. I touched the body. It didn't *feel* like a human.

Bored, I click through preservation articles and other taxidermy forums until I'm on a porn site. I try to be normal and jerk off to a happy woman with curly brown hair and a toothy grin. Her tits bounce, but her eyes—they glare at me. Pull me in and trap me. Holding me in a cell while millions of cameras watch my every move. Judging me.

A pop-up blocks the video. *The Pure Companion Company!* blinks at the top. An uncanny picture of a naked woman staring off into space fills the frame. *Real dolls for real fun!*

I lean closer to the screen. The eyes—the eyes are what stop me. Bleak, like a fish drying on a dock. Empty, like the salted crust at the bottom of a dried-up well. Dead, as if a man had just killed her.

Then I realize it's a fucking doll.

I click the advertisement and scan the website. In the reviews, the main complaint is the price—on average, it's ten grand a doll —but that seems reasonable when you flip through the gallery of the different models. Some of them look goddamn real, and on top of that, you can switch magnetic faces and opt into luxury pussy materials. It's surreal.

The skin. The skin is the hardest part. What would it *feel* like?

An idea instantly pops into my head. What if I used a sex doll as the mold for the Daughter?

I can add the doll's price to the Mother's invoice.

It takes some digging, but I finally find the Pure Companion Company's headquarters, which is only a couple of miles away.

The pop-up advertisement must have been targeted at me, being a local. At least, that's what I hope.

I turn to the freezer door. If I'm not here, I can't do anything to *it*.

I need to do this.

I drive to the outskirts of town and pull into a parking lot. To one side of the lot rests a large warehouse, painted cream. On the other side resides a multi-story building with reflective windows, like double-sided mirrors. I take my chances on the building.

Inside, the hum of electricity vibrates through the air. Each step on the tile sends an echo through the lobby. On the right, a man stands at a kiosk with his hands neatly folded in front of him. His black hair is slicked back, his cleft chin forward. His thin lips pull back into a smile, baring his teeth. A painted portrait of himself hangs on the wall behind him. *Founder, Owner, CEO* written at the bottom.

The Founder locks onto my gaze, his eye contact strong. I get the sense that he's been waiting for me for years now. As if he knows why I'm here.

"How can I help you today?" the Founder asks.

I sniff as I glance around the room. "Is this the Pure Companion Headquarters?"

"It is."

I crack my neck. "I want to see the products up close before I purchase one. Do you have any sample models?"

"None that you can *use*, I'm afraid," the Founder chuckles. "There are models you can touch in the back. With supervision, of course."

I nod and force out a chuckle that I hope sounds like a laugh, but it comes out garbled, like a tiny boy choking on his own spit.

The Founder doesn't move; his lips stay pulled into a tight smile. I pull at my collar, heat building in my temples.

This is going to be awkward. I should've emailed.

But then I'd have to wait for skin samples in the mail.

"Please," the Founder says, stepping around the kiosk and onto the main floor. "Let me show you our companions."

We walk across the lobby to a white door, down a corridor,

and into a room filled with sex dolls. Some stand, propped up with furniture pieces that resemble tripods, and other dolls sit on plastic chairs. Every doll is a different shade and shape. Naked. Their pussies bare. I snicker. I like fur on pussies; it's more natural—more primal—that way.

These dolls aren't for me; they're for a normal man. I've never been normal.

The dolls' eyes are cast down. I may not be like other men, but I can see the appeal in empty, unjudging eyes.

I touch one on the arm. A pleasant sensation instantly fills me. The skin is slightly textured. The bumps and grooves in the exterior are subtle, covered with a fine mesh of hair, as if meticulously implanted by hand with the loose strands of a child's eyebrow. There is a moistness to it too, like the doll put on lotion recently. The idea of stretch. Of limberness. It's almost real.

How the hell did he make a doll feel like human skin?

I doubt a dead epidermis will stretch around one of these dolls though. Still, it's worth asking.

"Have you tried putting one of these in latex?" I ask as I circle a set of black-haired dolls. Latex is the closest approximation to a human hide that I can think of. "Something tight?"

The Founder's smile fades into stoic concentration.

"Our Pure Companion's patented Skyn product is very close to human skin. Any preparatory measures you take with human skin must also be taken with Pure Companion Skyn."

I angle my chin. What is he getting at?

"Have you already purchased the outfit?" he asks.

I grimace. It's not like I can return the Daughter's hide and exchange it for a different size. "Yes?"

"Then order the doll a size smaller," the Founder adds. "It makes things easier."

We go through the process. The price tag comes to over eleven thousand dollars. I have the credit to purchase it.

Adding a surprise charge like that to the Mother's price tag, no matter how rich she is, won't go over well.

I tap my fingers on the counter. I should call the Mother. Confirm the purchase with her.

"I've got something for you," the Founder says.

He reaches under the counter, then he puts a pink bottle on the countertop. A mailing label sticks to the side with printed instructions: *Dilute 1:15 and rub into skin. DO NOT SWALLOW. May cause death.*

"This is the Founder's Secret Formula," he says mischievously.

I glance from his face up to the portrait behind him. He *is* the Founder.

"It helps keep the exterior surface natural," he explains. "It works well for humans too. It stops aging. As long as she's not allergic, it can make a woman's skin baby soft again."

Dolls *and* humans can use it?

"What's in it?" I ask.

He smirks. "I'm afraid I can't say exactly. It includes natural ingredients. Living materials. Think of it as organic." He pushes the bottle forward. "It's safe to use. Give it to your mother. Your daughter, even."

The Daughter.

My mouth runs dry. Images flash across my mind: my hands kneading the solution into the Daughter's skin. Those images swirl until I'm killing my own victim and rubbing the Secret Formula into her pussy *just* to preserve her in a similar state. To fuck and remember and relive her death any time I want.

I wrinkle my nose. It's too easy, though. There's something that the Founder is hiding.

"What's the catch?" I ask.

"It's a new blend of the product, and new products have testing phases," the Founder says cautiously. "I'll give you the Pure Companion—free of charge—*if* you're willing to use the Secret Formula. Give us an update in two weeks' time. I can have the manufacturing department add more bottles of the Secret Formula to your package when your Companion is ready. You can use the Secret Formula on the doll or on something else."

I can't use it on the doll. The doll is going inside of the Daughter's hide. And what does he mean by "something else"? Who would I give it to? *What* would I give it to? The Daughter?

I grimace, my jaw clenching in annoyance. *You're being paranoid,*

I lecture myself. *He doesn't know about the Daughter. Besides, you can't use a solution like that on a corpse. There's no use. It's already dead.*

But I can use it on something else. I can save it for someone new. It's not like the Founder will know.

"I'll use it on the doll," I lie.

CHAPTER 4

I DON'T LOOK AT THE BODY LIKE A WOMAN. IT'S A SPECIMEN. AN object to preserve. And with any specimen, there's the process of skinning it.

I remove the body from the cardboard box, then carry it to the metal table. The frozen body stares straight ahead like a marble statue with flat eyes sunken inside of the sockets. It's dusted with frozen crystals, like a pale piece of pork covered with frost. Freezer burn so beautiful, it resembles tiny diamonds.

It's easier to remove the skin when they're cold, not when they're frozen. The body thaws on the table while I connect the crane and metal hooks and move the furniture around until I have the right space marked out for the job. Next, I work the hook through the Daughter's Achilles tendon. It's hard to pierce. With some force, the metal anchors through the tissue.

The faint scent of cat fur and rotting fruit mixes in my nostrils, a familiar and pleasant perfume. I keep focused on that scent, concentrating on it as the crane hoists the body up.

The limbs dangle like a deer. Hair scrapes against the dirty cement floor, the blond strands glimmering in the dim light. The tits shift slightly with the suspension.

My eyes wander to the pussy.

The cold lips cling together with little beads of moisture

melting in the curled pubic hairs. The tendrils are darker there, a deep brown vastly different from the hair on the scalp, proving that the head hair is dyed. Even still, those pussy lips cling together like slices of frozen chicken in a plastic bag. If I'm not careful, I'll rip the skin, and with frays like that, it'll be hard to sew back.

But they'll be so goddamn tight.

I ignore the tension in my groin. This is work. Just work. Just another dead animal to stuff.

At the same time, I've never worked with an animal like this before. Most specimens have fur or feathers or even scales to hide the sewing seams, but not a human. I warned the Mother about this. I still need to do my best to hide the seams.

The feet are a decent option. Shoes can hide the reality.

I can hide the seams behind her pussy hair too.

Her pussy? No. Not *her* pussy. This is a dead body with no more identity than the cats and dogs I stuff regularly. *She* doesn't own anything, not even a pussy.

It's just a pussy.

I focus on the body, letting my hands wander down to the stomach. I'll have to pull the muscles and flesh out, and it won't be easy to pull it through the ankles. I'll have to cut open the abdomen. Maybe the ass too. Chopping it up and skinning it in smaller parts would be easier, but that means more seams. More wounds to hide.

The body droops with the increased temperature, the curves of the stomach loosening. A softness clings to the chilled specimen as my fingertips stumble over the spine, each bony bump like the pins of a music box.

If I only had heard her scream before she died.

My body tenses as hard as my dick, and I groan as the images flood my mind. I howl at myself. *Fucking focus!* It's a corpse. A job. A specimen. A product the Mother wants me to preserve.

The spine. The spine. *The spine.*

I'll cut along the spine.

"Work," I say out loud. My forefinger curls between the chilly cheeks of the ass, the pad of my finger skimming across the asshole.

"Seams," I breathe, my voice oozing with lust. My fingertip plays with those ridges, dew sliding across my fingertip. Cutting from asshole to the top of the spine makes the most sense.

My palms skim the inner thighs, the coolness of the skin like a gel pack thawing on the kitchen counter. And just as easily, my shoulders relax and I explore the body further. It's a real doll strung up, custom made for me. I reach between the thighs, careful to keep my distance from that icy clit.

That pinkish blue bead captures me. It pulsates in my vision, even though I know that's impossible. She's fucking dead. *It* is dead. And yet, it's like the blood rushed to the surface of the body as it died. Made the clit bulbous and hard, like the glass eye of a rat, pushed into a perfect cavern of clay. Like the bitch was fucked right as it took its last breath. Like it came hard, knowing that this was the last time.

I yank back. My chest is heavy. Heat burns in my temples. I scowl. A bitter tang fills my mouth, saliva pooling from my own inner disgust.

"It's not going to wake up. You're a stupid fucking pussy," I mutter to myself. "It's dead."

And a dead bitch can't hurt you.

The hair hangs like golden leaves from the branches of an autumn tree, and the breasts turn into snowy hills, ready to be kneaded back to life. Clay needs a little water. Frozen meat needs a bowl of water. But the Daughter? The body doesn't need water; it needs a hand. A warm hand. Even a warm, *rough* hand would massage some energy back into the body. It could even make the body feel like the bitch is fighting for it.

Impending doom wells inside of me, a hunger I know I won't be able to satiate, and yet I can't cool that voice, that knowledge that *this is it.* This is the closest I've been to my fantasy—fucking a woman that's dying—and yet, I know I can't do this. I shouldn't. I need to be good. Be normal. I need to live my life like a normal person under the radar. Normal people don't fuck dead girls like this.

But who would skin a perfectly good cunt without fucking it first?

The crane whines as I shift it in reverse. The body lowers to the ground. My fingers tap my side. I shouldn't be doing this. I know that. But no one can catch me here, and it's not like I killed it. It's already dead. And if I were dead, wouldn't I want to be used like this?

The Daughter's head hits the floor, knocking me out of my stupor. I grit my teeth; the trauma I may have caused is another annoyance to take care of, but hair can hide the damage, and there's no concern about concussions.

"I'm not a necrophiliac," I say.

But my dick is hard, screaming that I'm a liar.

I swear I'm not a freak. It's a dead body. A dead fucking body. That's it.

But who would I be if I didn't take advantage of an opportunity like this? A pliable body that won't tell me no. That won't fight back. That may not scream for me, but that doesn't matter. Not when I can't get in trouble for how rough I am with it.

Besides, if the Mother notices anything, it's not like she can go to the police. Her request for human taxidermy is illegal. And the Mother won't check the Daughter's pussy.

There's no way I can get caught for this.

The body lies on the ground. I leave the metal hooks on the ankles, the chains on the ground underneath it. I keep my eyes on the Daughter, tracing the limp body as I unzip my pants. I don't look away. The Mother may see her daughter, an extension of herself. I see perfection. An object has no real power. The perfect woman.

I stroke my cock, my fingertip rubbing over the urethral opening as I stare at the snowy valley between the cunt's legs. I reach toward the set of drawers and go to the bottom where I keep the lubricants. There's a warming gel, but part of me wants to savor the ice of the body. To experience something different. To understand why those necrophiliacs enjoy fucking corpses so much.

I'm not a necrophiliac. I know this about myself. Even if I am, I'm not *raping* a woman. It's a corpse. A useless, rotting body.

In all honesty, I'm giving it a purpose.

My knees scrape the brittle cement. I angle myself at the frozen cave. Then I grab the blond hair, my knuckles scratching the hard floor.

"Dead fucking bitch," I say.

My dick enters it. A chill runs through me—it's different to fuck a frozen cunt—but my dick softens. It's *not* enough. Not enough to know that it's dead. Not enough to know that it died tragically young. No, it's like fucking a frozen smoothie that's turned to an icy block, and I clench my jaw, angry at the stupid thing.

I finally did it. Finally got the nerve to fuck a corpse, and it has the nerve to resist giving me what I want?

I punch the head. The chin jerks to the side.

"Make a goddamn noise," I shout.

My mind shifts to the drawers where I keep the spare laptop. Quickly, I find it and click through until I'm on the dark web and downloading one of my favorite videos. I increase the volume, not caring if anyone can hear me through the garage door. People watch horror movies all the time, don't they? I'm not doing anything wrong. I need this. The screams start, and my dick comes back to life, and I look down at that body, hunger blooming in my chest. The whimpers fill my head and arousal spins through my thoughts.

I enter the pussy again.

Instantly, my mind transports me. We're in the snow. She's naked, and I'm clothed, because I found a lost cunt without a home. She shivers and claws through the icy ground to get away from me. I hold her still. Her pussy is rough and fucking frigid, but the lube lets my cock slide, and the friction—god damn it, that rough friction feels good. Feels like she's fighting me. Like she's desperate to escape, and I'm the Abominable Snowman.

I yank the head to the other side, the body cracking as the cold meat breaks, shifting into place for me, and I growl, the pleasure rushing to my head. The body is a victim now. *My* victim. And she's cold. Colder than a laptop powered on once a week for porn. Colder than a thawing rat in a snake's cage. Colder than a dead cunt tucked away in a freezer.

The chill embraces me, and my throat tightens.

"Dead little cunts love getting fucked," I say, my voice hoarse. "Don't they?"

I open my eyes and lean on my elbows, staring into those cloudy blue eyes. The deep greens come out, and for a second, she's not the Daughter, not even a corpse. She's dying, and I'm killing her. She's mine.

I explode inside the pussy, the groan ripping through me as pleasure bursts from my seams, pulling me apart from the inside out. I come so hard, my vision turns to snow. It's better than my hand. Better than any of the cock sleeves I've used. Better than fucking a willing woman.

When I blink, coming back to reality, I focus on the hair. The Daughter's blond hair is tinted brown from the blood and clay layered thick on the garage floor. A new sensation curls inside of me. It curls to the surface and broadens my shoulders.

The dead cunt lies on the floor like a doll tossed aside, the neck contorted in an odd angle, as if it has a broken neck. I'd never do that to a cunt; a broken neck is too easy. Too quick.

I pull out of the thawed pussy hole, then wipe my hands on a stained rag. I've got to skin it soon, and with the Pure Companion being delivered any day now, I can't keep messing around.

I start the crane again. The body sways in the air. I take the knife, splitting it from the asshole, down the spine, to the nape of the neck. The skin splits apart, exposing the mangled fringes of muscles and rib bones, and I see myself. All humans are the same underneath, and yet, I know we *aren't* the same.

The Daughter is dead. I'm alive.

Saliva pools on my tongue as I pull the skin from the muscle. The blood stretches like cheese from a grilled sandwich. A sandwich can be pulled apart. A laptop can be broken down piece by piece. Even humans can split from their skin.

A scream from the snuff film breaks into my thoughts, and that's when I realize I *want* to preserve this specimen. In the end, I can't deny that it's a beautiful object, and I owe it to myself. After all, I'm the best in the region.

But if I preserve the body, I'll use it again. And that will make it a habit.

I'm not a necrophiliac.

"Who the fuck cares?" I say.

No one answers back. Because no one will know about what I'm doing with the Daughter. An object can't speak. An object is simply owned.

And god damn it, I own that body right now.

CHAPTER 5

A HUMAN HIDE IS A FUNNY THING. NO MATTER HOW GENTLE YOU are, it grays. It dulls. It loses its luster.

The Mother knows this. I told her this. *I know this.*

I don't give a shit about the Mother. Not really. A product is a product. She can go write a one-star review. I don't care.

It's my own reaction that bothers me. Confusion pulses inside of me and grips my temples like a vise.

Why am I disappointed?

The pink bottle, the only bright color in a garage full of browns and grays, mocks me. The Founder said it was a secret formula to help preserve doll and human skin. Who comes up with this bullshit?

Yet, my fingers curl into themselves. How much lotion—or whatever the fuck it is—would've helped preserve the Daughter's texture? How much would have made the body *feel* like a living, breathing victim?

I open the bottle and sniff the pearl-colored cream. It's bitter at first, then slightly sweet. Like ammonia diluted with sugar and water.

Baby soft, the Founder had said.

A while later, the Pure Companion arrives in a tall box, similar to the cardboard coffin. Contrary to the Daughter, the doll is wrapped in a plastic bag and covered with pink tissue paper like a gift. My head fills with images of pornstars pulling on latex outfits, a plastic layer so tight that it molds to the body like scales.

That kind of costuming used to do something for me. Seeing the pornstar try desperately to put it on. Struggling to fit. Like a prisoner caught in quicksand, sinking to their own demise. *Helpless.*

I used to watch those kinds of videos often before I moved on to more…violent videos.

Sitting on the floor of the garage, I pull the doll into my lap. The Daughter's hide wrinkles on the floor next to me like a deflated balloon, except for the toes. The toes are rigid with cotton and clay. I couldn't remember if the Pure Companions had individual toes, and I wasn't sure I wanted to stretch the hide that far.

I glance at the doll's feet, then take scissors and cut off the silicone toes. They drop to the floor like peeled grapes.

I pull the hide around the feet, and it gets caught around the plastic calf. It's too snug. Like most animals, the skin has shrunken, grown tougher, and it's like ringing a child's size latex glove onto an octopus's tentacle. Nothing fits. You have to force it into place, and even then, it's like it has a will of its own. It won't submit without a fight.

Sweat gathers on my brow as I struggle to get the doll inside of the skin. With other specimens, you have options that make it easier. Mounts for the foam or plastic. I can hook the silicone body onto the crane, but the plastic ankles may not be strong enough to hold the weight. I can always use clay to repair any ripped materials, but it's a personal challenge now. A way to prove that *I'm* the one in control here.

So I twist. I shove. I wrestle that rubbery plastic body against the shriveled skin, and I huff like an aggravated dog and shimmy the thing into place. The skin is like fabric at this point. A raw material that isn't doing its job to costume the doll.

Eventually, I get most of the human leather into place, and after I add clay to where the Daughter needs more shape, I begin sewing the seams. The weight rests on my lap, and that deep sensation fills me. I'm back to when the Daughter had cold skin. When I could still enter its body and pretend that I was fucking a woman to death in the snow.

The Daughter's muscles rest in large chunks in the walk-in freezer. I'll have to figure out what to do with the meat soon. If I chop up the flesh small enough, the veterinarian clinic won't notice. They handle my animal cremation. Human flesh isn't that different.

I manipulate the body until the head is in my lap. With a flat-head screwdriver, I tuck the folds of the eyelids into the sockets around the blue glass eyes. I do the same with the pussy folds until all of those layers stack up like deli meat.

Once it's finished, I lie it down, then stand, gazing at the specimen. The hide clings to the rubber doll, like a snake shedding flaking scales. The eyes are too small, like the Daughter is part human, part rat. I should've used boar eyes. I could've used more clay to bring the glass to the surface.

I carry the specimen over my shoulder like a sack of rice, hoping the bedroom scenery will make it look more realistic.

It's the same. The hide is shriveled, and I'm left with a thing that resembles a giant naked mole rat.

"Or a fucking alien," I mutter.

Irritation prickles my skin until my hair stands on end. Why can't I do this? Why can't I make the corpse resemble the Daughter? I'm the best in the region. How can the best fail? It's disgusting. It's like I'm preventing myself from reaching my goal, because I know what it means once I'm done.

And if I never finish?

If the Mother doesn't want the Daughter anymore, perhaps I can keep it. Work on it. Perfect it.

But that won't be enough. I want the Daughter to be *alive*. I want to imagine she's dying right in front of me.

This… This thing lying on the floor will never be that.

And that itch starts to grow. The desire to learn. To practice. To perfect my craft until I have something better.

The doorbell rings.

For the first time in years, the intrusion doesn't upset me.

Instead, I think of the potential on the other side of the door. A new customer. A shift in focus. More raw materials. Perhaps all I need is a different project to find the inspiration to fix the Daughter.

My jaw relaxes. I walk through the hallway to the front door.

CHAPTER 6

Heat builds in my cheeks as I near the front door. If it's the Mother, I'll rip the bandaid and show her what a freak her precious little girl has become.

I swing open the door.

A young woman stands on the porch. Empty-handed. A smile on her lips.

What the fuck?

"Hey," she says. "I locked my keys and phone in my car." She shrinks behind her shoulders. "I'm a genius, I know. Can I borrow your phone? I've got to get a locksmith out here."

I blink. A woman is standing in front of me, asking for help. My tongue grows wet with drool. I shove my hand in my pocket, right by my smartphone. She needs it from me. I should give it to her. It's what I *should* do.

"I'm sorry," she says. "I should've introduced myself. I'm your neighbor. I live next door. I moved in last winter?"

I check the street; we're alone.

"Right," I say. I straighten my shoulders, then force a smile. "Sorry. No cell phone. But I've got a landline."

I step to the side, giving her a view of the house. Her shoulders tense as she takes in the darkness behind me, then her lips subtly shift as she glances around, those internal bells warning her to stay away from a man like me. The subconscious desire for survival. The need for someone to tell her to stop. To run away before I catch her.

"Come on in," I say, waving her inside. "I'll grab it for you. It's cordless."

"Thanks. I'll stay out here."

I chuckle. The Neighbor is smart, but not smart enough.

"The phone doesn't work out here," I counter. "Trust me, I've tried. The reception is terrible. You have to come inside."

Her body goes rigid. I hunch my shoulders and make myself smaller. My impression of a harmless loner. Someone insignificant.

"Once the phone call is done, you can wait outside. I'll wait with you," I offer.

She shivers, then shakes her head. "It's just you never know these days, do you?" She laughs nervously, then steps inside. "Thanks so much for your help."

"You're right," I say. "You can never be too careful."

I close the front door behind us.

The Neighbor is instantly drawn to a black bear, standing on its hind legs in the front room. She gawks at it in awe.

"Wow," she says. "This is really good." She tilts her head to the side. "It's scary good. Do you collect taxidermy?"

"No. It's what I do."

She nods, then travels from piece to piece, marveling at them like works of art.

I should feel bad for what I know is coming. The hunger inside of me widens, spreading itself around my core like the arms of an impenetrable beast. I can't fight it any longer.

"How long have you been doing taxidermy?" she asks.

My brain drifts off as I stare at the closed curtains by the front window. No one saw her come in here.

The Neighbor's big brown eyes peek up at me. My fists coil with frustration. If she had opened her eyes a little more, she would've known that those red flags she saw were *not* ones to ignore. Maybe then I'd have a proper fight.

I'm not insignificant.

"A long time," I say. "I'll get you that phone."

I head to the garage. My heart pounds in my ears. This is different. This is a bad fucking idea. If I leave her alone, she'll see the Daughter. She'll tell the police. And when the police come, I'll be arrested.

I have no choice now. I know what I have to do. My eyes wander the garage, searching for the crowbar.

She's in the front room, not your bedroom, my mind corrects, that tiny part of me that knows this is wrong. That society will never let me forget something like this.

The Neighbor is not a threat. She's just a woman who needs to borrow my phone. She doesn't deserve to die.

But god, that body will look so good with its legs spread, the life fleeing from those brown eyes.

My dick tents my pants, a pre-cum stain drooling through the fabric. I clutch my bulge and groan at myself to calm down.

You're making a mistake, I think. *This isn't about protecting yourself. It's about everything else that comes with it.*

I find the crowbar. I even grab a pocket knife and sharpen it quickly. My chest expands as I think of the process. Of the exact things I want to do.

I'll knock her out. I won't kill her. Not right then. Not until I'm deep inside of her.

Then I'll use the knife.

I open the garage door and find her outside of the master bedroom, her hands quaking by her sides.

"What…is…that?!" she whispers.

Rage flares in my skull. She's invading my space.

She swings around, and I hit her in the head with the crowbar. She falls to the ground.

I unzip my pants quickly and drop the crowbar. I pull down her pants and yank off one leg, then toss her onto her stomach so I can take the bitch from behind. I lift her hips as I angle myself at her pussy. My dick scrapes against the dry folds, and so I spit in my hand, pushing the palm to her slit.

She stirs, sniffling awake. Her eyes flutter as she looks over her

AUDREY RUSH

shoulder. She screams and crawls away, and I angle myself on top
of her, using my body weight to hold her down. She cries, then
grabs one of the pedestals. It crashes into my head, and she rolls
to the side. Her eyes are frantic. Looking around. Desperate for an
escape.

I grab the crowbar again, anger flooding my veins.

"Get away from me!" the Neighbor screams.

I wrestle her until she's flat on the ground, then I pinch her
nose and mouth closed, and she convulses. It's not enough to keep
me out. I shove my cock inside of her, and she's hot. A fucking
furnace. And it's suffocating. But then she squeezes me, strangling
my cock with her tight, frightened pussy, and it's like I'm in the
abyss and I don't care about the heat. I thrust my hips. The rancid
scent of her fear stinks up the air, and I fuck her harder. Tears roll
down her face.

"Please," she begs in a muffled voice. "Don't hurt me."

And those eyes, so full of water, a muddy brown, *should* make
me feel something. Should make me feel guilt. Sympathy.
Anything. They don't.

My dick throbs as I place the crowbar against her neck and
pin it against her throat so she can't breathe, and her cunt sheaths
me. The heat builds as she struggles, and I fight to keep her still.
Her body pulses. Tightens. A sleeve of skin that's mine. All
fucking mine.

"Pluu—" she gurgles.

I lean on the crowbar with one hand and whip out the knife
with the other. I stab it into her mouth and nail her tongue to the
back of her mouth. Blood gushes from her face hole, and I keep
pumping inside of her. Her brown eyes widen, and as I pull out
the knife, they shut.

I bring the knife to her neck and I cut. The blood oozes
around me, metal ripe in the air, and it's cliche, but I don't care: I
fuck that bloody gash on her neck. I don't even feel the warmth.
I'm transfixed by the life fading from her eyes.

"Beg me," I beckon. "Beg me not to kill you."

Her eyelids flutter, then stop, and her chin turns to the side.
She can't say a goddamn thing.

34

And I come.

When the convulsions subside, I roll to my side and stare up at the ceiling. The air conditioning kicks on, waving cold air across my damp skin, and I realize I'm covered in blood.

I sit up and hold my breath as I face the body. The slit throat. The bloody mouth. Even after that chaos, one pant leg still clothes the body.

The Neighbor was young. She might have been dating. There might even be a family that still wants her around.

I wait for those emotions to come. The guilt. The remorse.

My mind works faster than that. I'm a practical man. I contemplate the important details that I need to acknowledge now.

No one saw her come into my house. I made sure of that. And with her phone locked in her car, there's no way she could've told anyone she was coming here.

What I did was wrong. I know that. But I was good for a long time. I stayed away from others. I kept to the animals and put my passion into stuffing creatures that were already dead. I only killed things when life was extremely difficult. And that was only animals, things without real intelligence. And after I found the snuff films, I didn't even need that anymore.

What I did was self-defense. The Neighbor would've told the police, and it would've looked like a crime, as if I had done something bad to the Daughter, when the Daughter was a corpse long before it came here.

I didn't kill the Daughter.

I stand up and stretch my hands above my head. I walk through the house lazily, taking my time before I move on to the next step.

In the garage, the pink bottle shines like a pearl inside of an oyster. The fountain of youth tucked into a bottle of plastic.

The usual methods don't work for human hides. I'll have to order another doll too.

It's worth a shot.

I scoop up the Neighbor and take it to the garage, lying it on the metal table. The police will do a welfare check soon. In a big city like this, people disappear all the time. I can get rid of the flesh and bones like the other animals, like I was planning on doing with the Daughter anyway. Eventually, the police will lose interest. The Neighbor isn't special.

The Neighbor is an object.

CHAPTER 7

WEEKS PASS. THEN THE PHONE CALLS START. I NEVER PICK UP. One day, the Mother switches to texts.

When will she be done? she asks.

Even though I expect the messages now, they still annoy me. Perhaps it's that lack of understanding I have with a blood connection. In my experience, two people may copulate and give you life, but that doesn't mean that there's any devotion between you.

Soon, I respond. It's the only answer that will get her to shut up.

In reality, the Daughter is done. I could redo the specimen, but that seems like a waste of time when I know the hide will break apart like egg shells. It's a mess, but it's probably the best the Daughter will get. I should honestly get rid of the Daughter and be done with the whole thing.

I don't do anything. The Daughter sits on the folding chair in the master bedroom, the crumbling skin of the tits flaking as I touch it. Like candied slices of an orange peel. It's motivation, I suppose. A transition. Proof that even an expert like me can still improve. You can always learn to do better.

The Mother will come to pick her up soon, and then I'll have to decide what to say. What to do with her.

The Neighbor lies on my bed, propped up like it's watching television. Black panties stretch across the cunt. The tits are bare, those perky bells hanging down, the nipples permanently puckered and stuffed with clay. A sewn cut decorates the neck like a dangly red necklace. The Neighbor's mouth hangs open—crusty white liquid dripping from the lips.

I should clean it. Fucking the mouth hole and pretending like we're reliving that same death moment makes me come, but it doesn't *satisfy* me.

The Neighbor is better than the Daughter, but it's not what I want. I have no use for keeping lifelike human bodies in my house. It's the process that I like. The ritual of the hunt. The chase. The fucking. Skinning and stuffing are part of it too, but it's the start of the journey that holds me close and draws me back for more.

"Just keep fucking it," I tell myself as I stare at the Neighbor. "You don't need to kill anyone else."

No matter how much I say those words, my mind won't listen.

The solution is almost gone now. I'll need to contact the Founder soon and see if he's willing to give me more. I'll have to lie and say that I ended up giving it to someone else, like he suggested. Maybe my mother. I'll have to come up with an excuse as to why I ordered a second doll, just in case he asks.

Perhaps a man like that knows better than to ask questions.

I squirt the last pump of the Secret Formula into my hand, the creamy white gel cold in my palm. I rub it into the Neighbor's skin while paying special attention to the tits, but I find myself squeezing so hard that the silicone divots under my fingertips.

"Making a fucking noise," I growl.

The doorbell chimes through the house. A fist pounds on the front door.

The Mother.

I throw the comforter over the Neighbor, then go to the front of the house. It's time to get this over with. I'm done waiting. I've got to move on.

I fling open the door and broaden my shoulders. The Mother pushes me aside, knocking into me once again. This time, her warmth isn't an invasion. I welcome it.

I grin at the back of her head.

"Where is she?" the Mother asks. She stomps through the house and glares at the specimens as if she'll discover the Daughter propped up among them. Her face screws up, and she pulls off her blazer in frustration. Her arms are still bumpy, but they're a light pink now, not nearly as red as before.

With enough care—with more Secret Formula—even her body can be useful. It can stave off the hunger.

For a while.

"Have you finished it yet?" she barks.

It. The Mother has finally made the transition to seeing the Daughter for the lifeless doll it really is. An object. Nothing more. The Mother's eyebrow lifts, her upper lip curling.

"Back here," I say. I motion toward the hallway. The Mother glares at me, then turns back to the open front door. The same SUV waits on the curb.

I close the front door, tucking us inside. Her shoulders tense. She steps forward with confidence though, her red heels tapping on the floor like the hands in a clock.

"I just want to see an update," she says. "Is that too much to ask?"

I let her talk. Customers—whether it's for hunted game, a beloved pet, or a dead daughter—know what they want, and they often act like they're entitled to an expedited process. The superiority grates on me. I'm not cocky enough to think I'm better than them. I know what I am. What we are.

Animals.

Objects.

Meat and skin.

A vein pulses in the side of the Mother's neck, and a familiar sensation grows inside of me. I should've jerked off before I answered the door.

Jerking off wouldn't have been enough though, but I know what *will* be enough now.

My dick hardens. I follow the Mother into the master bedroom and grab the crowbar off of the dresser, holding it behind my back. The knife waits in my pocket, ready for use.

39

The Daughter, sitting in the folding chair, is the first thing the Mother sees. The Mother's hands ball into fists.

My cock pushes through the hole in my boxers and twitches against the metal zipper of my pants. A fraction of pain sizzles inside of me.

"What did you do?" the Mother whispers. She spins around, her face pulled back into a snarl. "You ruined her!"

"You knew there was a risk that it wouldn't turn out the way you—"

Her eyes stop on the bed.

"Is someone sleeping in here?" she whispers. Her hand clutches her chest. She inches forward, and I readjust my grip on the crowbar.

"Not someone," I say.

"Why didn't you—"

Then she pulls back the comforter.

Her body freezes. The Neighbor, a hybrid human and rubber doll, lies in front of the Mother. She touches the Neighbor's mouth, my brittle come grazing her fingertips.

The Mother turns, her jaw dropped. Fear clouds her eyes, her lips trembling.

"Y-y-you killed her," she stammers. "H-he said you weren't like that."

He? Who is he?

"It's just a doll," I say calmly. "You can't kill a doll."

She clenches her jaw. "You're a monster!"

The Mother lunges forward, and adrenaline pumps through me as her clawed fingers dig into my shoulders. She trips on the comforter, and I shove her dumb ass into the ground. She crawls like a rodent, and I laugh maniacally, stomping on the back of her calves until she stops. I didn't even need the crowbar this time.

I pull the knife from my pocket and flick it open. The Mother flips over, backing away like a crab. I tap the flat edge of the blade against my palm.

"John!" she screams. She looks for the front door. "My husband! He's—"

I lurch on top of her and cover her mouth. She punches my

nose. Anger surges through me, and I don't care about my raging dick anymore. I want the bitch dead. Before she speaks another word, I kneel down and slice her throat, this time right under her head where the neck folds. I cut with purpose, knowing that this is the best way to hide the seams.

Blood spouts from her like a fountain of ecstasy, and the Mother falls silent.

I crawl on top of her limp body and rub my dick through my pants. Irritation simmers inside of me. I let it cool. Her blond hair is matted with blood, and her neck is limp now.

It's a waste. A goddamn waste to let her die without fucking her.

But it came so easily this time.

There's potential in the Mother. Even if she has bumpy arms and an old cunt, I'm not going to waste raw material. Hell, I'll pull the first doll out of the Daughter and use it with the Mother's skin. After all, the Mother gave the Daughter life, and that debt should be repaid.

I drag the body by the feet to the garage. The walk-in freezer is empty, and now that I've gotten rid of the Neighbor's and the Daughter's flesh, I'm not concerned with the outcome of this situation. The police stopped questioning me about the Neighbor a long time ago. And with the Mother, there's no trail of the Mother coming here, since our agreement was illegal.

I situate the body in the freezer when the doorbell rings.

I stop and listen. My heart races.

Maybe I'm not in the clear. Maybe someone heard the Mother scream, and they've called the police. The Mother was a loud bitch. I'll need a good explanation for that. A television show, perhaps. It's all so violent these days. Society is hypocritical. They think snuff is bad, when the average viewer watches computer-generated death every single day.

I seal the freezer shut with the new padlock. My shoulders lift, ready to sigh in relief.

A trail of blood leads back to the master bedroom.

The doorbell rings again.

I'm fucked.

No, I remind myself. *I'm a taxidermist. Blood spills sometimes. It's part of the job.*

The doorbell rings a third time, and I stand in the hallway outside of the bedroom. I click through my phone to the surveillance footage. On the porch, a man in a suit runs a hand through his black hair.

"Jane?" he asks. He knocks again. "Mr. Wright, I'm looking for my wife. Jane, are you in there?"

I peek through the peephole in the front door to get a better view. Past the man, the Mother's SUV still waits on the curb. The engine is off now.

It's the Father.

CHAPTER 8

THE BELL CHIMES THROUGH THE HOUSE FOR A FOURTH TIME. I open up the door slowly, the hinges creaking. I hold my breath.

If I have to, I can kill the Father too.

I *have* to kill him. It's survival now.

I lift my eyes, meeting the Father. A familiarity takes hold of me, and I squint and try to place him.

His hair is slicked back, his eyes dark, and the stiffness of his shoulders reminds me of someone. His lips pull back, his mouth forming a perfect smile.

Then I realize who he is.

The Founder.

"Mr. Wright," he says. He offers his hand to me. "Good to see you again."

I look down at my hand, blood drying in the webs between my fingers.

I shake his hand.

"Are they inside?" he asks.

They. He means his wife. The Mother. *And* the Daughter.

"My wife hired you to take care of our daughter," he says matter-of-factly, a hint of excitement in his tone. "Are they in there?"

He knew, then. When I came to the Pure Companion Company headquarters, he *knew*.

"They are," I say. My skin crawls. I don't understand what his purpose is, and I don't like being taken advantage of. This feels like a trap. Like he knew this is what I would do. Like he wanted me to kill his wife for him. Like he wants to frame his murders on me.

I stir myself from those thoughts. *No.* That would be insane. There's no way he wanted to kill his own family and preserve them like mannequins for display.

"You called me for more of the Secret Formula. It must be working well then, Mr. Wright?"

The pink bottle.

I hold my arm out and step to the side like I did with his wife, giving the Founder access to the house. My pulse drums in my ears. This won't be easy. The Founder—the Father—is different from the others. He's a big man. My only advantage over him is that I have experience killing. I'm not afraid of murder.

But the Founder of the Pure Companion Company has *power,* and that power can ruin me. I can kill—I know that—but if I anger someone like him, what will he do? What is he capable of? Is there some higher power beyond him that will come back for justice?

Is this my last chance?

You killed his wife, my brain shouts. *He doesn't need the Daughter. He needs his fucking wife. He's going to kill you now too, unless you defend yourself.*

That's all it is. Self-defense. No one can blame me for that.

The Founder enters the master bedroom, his eyes passing over the Daughter in the folding chair and landing on the Neighbor lying in the bed. He steps closer, his eyes glued to the perfect body. He squeezes the Neighbor's hand, testing the skin. Blood whirls in my eardrums. I pull the pocketknife out, ready to strike.

He shifts to the Daughter.

In a daze, the Founder bends down, his spine angled like the branches of a willow tree. His nose skims the clumped hair, and he sucks in that scent, inhaling it like it's the only air he needs.

What does he smell? Is the jasmine shampoo still there, lingering in the dirty strands?

The Founder kneels down in front of the Daughter. The familiar rattle of a zipper whispers through the room. The feverish contact of skin against skin.

I peer around his side.

He's jerking off.

Within a few seconds, he comes into his palm, ammonia potent in the air. He rubs it on the Daughter's pussy, massaging the crumbling folds, as if it'll give the hide more life.

He wipes his palm on his pants, then stands. He faces me.

"Make my wife and daughter like the other one," he says, nodding toward the Neighbor. He pulls out his wallet and hands me several hundred-dollar bills. "I'll pay the rest when you finish. Once I see the final products, we can discuss our future business together."

The money flutters to the ground and mingles with the trail of blood. I stiffen. Fear tingles in my chest.

He's a predator circling me.

For a second, I stay still.

"Do we have a deal?" the Founder asks.

He bows his head slightly, and instinctively, I know there's a kinship between us. Two men, knowing exactly the kind of opportunity we have. The money we'll make. The bodies we'll use.

"When the Mother is done, we can discuss our business," I agree.

"I'll have more Secret Formula delivered tomorrow," he says. "You may have to use extra on my wife. She had sensitive skin."

Images of the Mother's red arms fill my head. It must have been a rash from an earlier version of the Secret Formula.

The Founder's steps rumble through the house. He stops at the front door, then turns to me. An unreadable expression covers his face. It's not nostalgic or even remorseful for what's happened. There's an acknowledgment there, like he knows me. Accepts me. A smile that says he has those unspeakable needs inside of his brain too.

"It's better like this," he says. It takes a minute, but I realize he's comforting me. Reassuring me that I shouldn't feel guilty about my needs. For what I've done.

The cunts I'll kill.

The hybrid dolls he'll sell.

The pussies we'll fuck.

He steps onto the front porch and closes the door behind him. His words stick with me, replaying in my ears: *It's better like this.* Not her. Not them. *It.* The words feel like they've been ripped from my own mind.

I go to the garage and begin cleaning the space, preparing it for the next specimen.

He's right. It is better this way.

CHAPTER 9

OVER THE YEARS, THE PROCESS IS PERFECTED. WE FIND OUR arrangement.

I don't stay in the house—too many witnesses to consider in a big city like that—but the Founder gladly gives me a signing bonus that's big enough to buy a new house in the countryside, surrounded by woods and a lake. It's a hassle to bring the flesh to the nearest veterinary clinic, and I still have to work with pet clients to ward off suspicion, but it's worth it to have enough privacy and space to chase the dumb cunts.

That will change soon. The Founder says he's working with a new type of client to get rid of the excess flesh—a culinary endeavor, if you will. And when the time comes, I'll be paid accordingly. No part of the raw material will go to waste.

A truck pulls up. The driver—a young man in a baseball cap —laughs causally as he parks the vehicle. A redhead leans out the open window, a bright smile on her lips as she takes in the beauty of the woods.

I agree with her. The woods are perfect. The cunts think they can escape me, but there's no use. Not when I own hundreds of acres in each direction.

At first, I thought the signing bonus was too much, but the Founder knew our products' worth. On the dark web, anything can be sold. A man will sell his soul if it gives him the object he wants. I understand that now.

The man in the baseball cap glances through the trees, not seeing me, but knowing I'm there. The Founder hires a few different men across the country to rent out vacation properties and wait until the right guests come along. Couples who are alone, or a young college student on spring break, or even a man taking a trip abroad before he settles down into domestic life. International tourists make for especially good products. The clients like the novelty, and as a company, we benefit from the lack of connection between the countries. You can report a missing person all you want, but it doesn't mean they'll be found. Eventually, everyone loses interest. After all, a missing body is a missing object. And with no body to be found, there's no crime.

The Founder gives the hirees an older version of the Secret Formula. With too high of a dose, it kills them right away, but with a micro dose, they're disoriented for a while. Part of our business agreement is that *I* get to kill them. So those hirees drop off the drugged prisoners in the woods and leave them to fend for their lives.

But every once in a while, one of the hirees takes an interest in a future hide. He fucks her. Brings her here. Tells her that he rented this house in the countryside or that he's borrowing it from his uncle. By nightfall, he disappears to get takeout from town, and I start my favorite part of the process.

I hunt them. Take what I want. Fuck them unconscious, ramming their bodies into the ground.

Then I kill them as I come.

Luckily, washing the bodies and lotioning them with the Secret Formula prevents any damage to the skin. It also puts me into work mode so that I'm ready to stuff them with the Pure Companion molds. Stuffing them isn't my favorite part, but it's the end of the ritual, and it refreshes me. It gives me appreciation for the next product.

It turns out that I wasn't the first taxidermist the Founder hired. I don't ask about my predecessor. It doesn't matter what happened to him, her, them, or *it*. Business is business, and as long as I get to fuck the little cunts, I don't care about what happened to the employee before me. It's not like I did anything to them.

As for the Founder, he continues to test the final products and gives them each their own individual names to capture their essence. There's a finesse to naming pocket pussies stuffed into silicone dolls with the texture of a real human skin. *Baby Doll. Kendra. Elise. Mindy.*

And we profit.

The redheaded woman stretches her arms, probably sore from the long car ride. She doesn't see me staring at her through the trees.

I don't feel bad for the redhead. In fact, I don't mourn any of them, nor do I feel guilty for what I'm about to do. In my mind, the bitch is already dead.

Denying my orgasm won't save her life.

ALSO BY AUDREY RUSH

———

EROTIC HORROR

Psychological

Standalone

My Girl

———

DARK ROMANCE

Stalker

Standalone

Crawl

Dead Love

Grave Love

Hitch

Assassin

The Feldman Brothers Duet

His Brutal Game

His Twisted Game

Mafia

The Adler Brothers Series

Dangerous Deviance

Dangerous Silence

Dangerous Command

Secret Society

The Marked Blooms Syndicate Series

Broken Surrender

Broken Discipline

Broken Queen

Secret Club

The Dahlia District Series

Ruined

Shattered

Crushed

Ravaged

Devoured

The Afterglow Series

His Toy

His Pet

His Pain

Billionaire

Standalone

Dreams of Glass

ACKNOWLEDGMENTS

Thank you to my amazing beta readers: Ashley, Jenni, Johanna, Lesli, and Marianne! You helped make this story the wonderfully messed up reality that it is! Thank you to my copy editor, Jackie at PR Publishing Group; you knock it out of the park every time. Thank you to my husband, Kai, for being an amazing graphic designer and supporting the transformation of these nightmares into stories. Thank you to my ARC readers for your honest reviews; you have no idea how much you help a book launch, and I'm so grateful that you were willing to take a chance on my first horror story! (And a special thanks to Bearded Dom, Lana, Lauren, Ryssa Elyse, and the Eclectic Editor for catching my typos!) And thank you to my daughter, Emma, for tolerating my writing sprints during screen time and being such a good kid at school.

But most of all, thank you to my readers. You are the reason I love to turn my daydreams and nightmares into books. I'm endlessly grateful for your support.

ABOUT THE AUTHOR

Audrey Rush writes kinky dark romance and erotic horror. She lives in Florida with her husband and daughter. She writes during school.

TikTok: @audreyrushbooks
Instagram: audreyrushbooks
Reader Group: bit.ly/rushreaders
Threads: @audreyrushbooks
Reader Newsletter: bit.ly/audreysletters
Amazon: amazon.com/author/audreyrush
Website: audreyrush.com
Facebook: fb.me/audreyrushbooks
Goodreads: author/show/AudreyRush
Email: audreyrushbooks@gmail.com

Printed in Great Britain
by Amazon